THE CHRISTMAS SPIDERS

5.5" x 8.5" (13.97 x 21.59 cm)
Full Color on White paper
Published by EMBER PRESS
ISBN-13: 978-0692347454 (Custom)
ISBN-10: 0692347453

emberpress.com

Book design and text composition by Ember Press
Story written by Angela Yuriko Smith
Illustrations by Robin Wiesneth

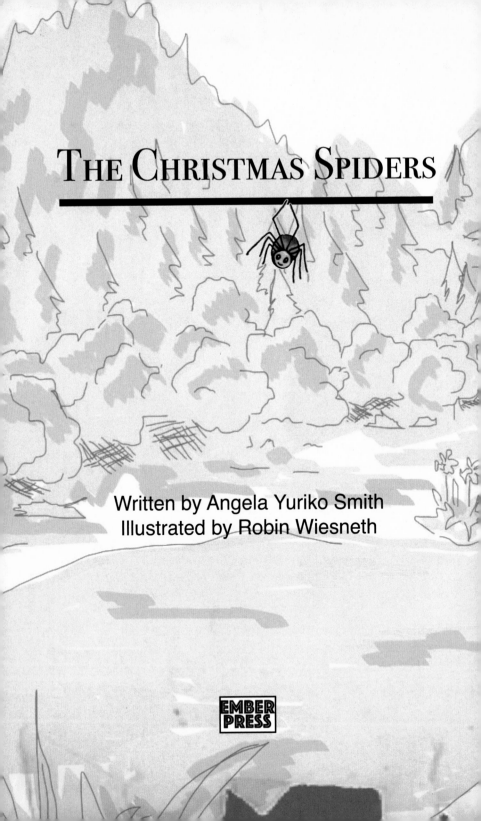

THE CHRISTMAS SPIDERS

Written by Angela Yuriko Smith
Illustrated by Robin Wiesneth

EMBER PRESS

There once lived a kind, old woman who had a great respect and love for all things living. One New Year's Day, she decided she wanted to write a book to teach others to love the world, so she packed up her paper and ink, kissed her family good bye for a year and moved into an abandoned little cabin she knew of at the top of a mountain at the edge of a thick forest.

She made herself a desk out of an old crate on the porch and would sit outside all day, working on her book with a view of the whole world spread out beneath her. Spiders lived underneath the crate, but the old woman found that if she didn't bother them they treated her likewise, and they kept away the flies that distracted her while she tried to think.

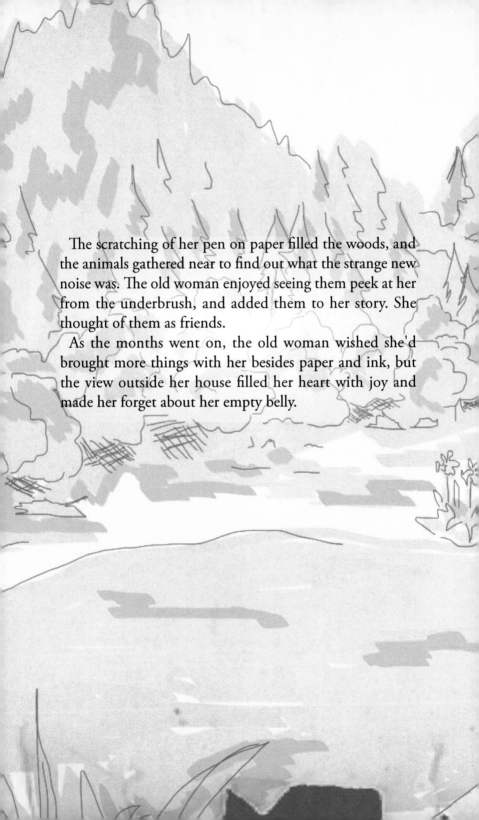

The scratching of her pen on paper filled the woods, and the animals gathered near to find out what the strange new noise was. The old woman enjoyed seeing them peek at her from the underbrush, and added them to her story. She thought of them as friends.

As the months went on, the old woman wished she'd brought more things with her besides paper and ink, but the view outside her house filled her heart with joy and made her forget about her empty belly.

Though she barely had food enough for herself, she always managed to leave a few crusts of bread out for the birds. In return, they kept hungry bugs away from the small vegetable garden she planted.

She left the peelings from her vegetables out for the deer and in return they kept the brush away from her house so forest fires couldn't come near. She let the weeds have a place by her well and in return they provided her with herbs for her tea and spices for her dinner. The old woman learned that the more she helped the world, the more it helped her.

In late spring, a pine sapling sprang up through the floor-boards of her little cabin and the kind, old woman didn't cut it down. Instead she moved her couch to give it room. The tree grew next to her window, and it made the woman happy to think that they both shared the light and the view.

All through the summer the little tree grew along with the old woman's book. During the late afternoons the woman would bring water to the tree, since it grew under her roof where the rain wouldn't reach, and read to the tree what she had written. The old woman shared the wise things she learned from watching the animals around her cabin. The tree flourished as it listened.

When autumn came, the afternoons grew chilly and the nights cold. One day she found a spider curled up, nearly frozen, in a corner on her porch. She brought the spider into her house, and placed it in the tree where it could live warm.

She began watching out for the frozen spiders on her porch and brought them all inside.

When winter came, food grew scarcer for the old woman and the animals that shared the woods with her, but she knew her year alone on the mountain was nearing its end. Her book had grown thick while her pile of blank paper had gotten thin.

The old woman was looking forward to seeing her children and grandchildren again, but she worried about what would happen to the birds when she no longer left her crusts and the deer without her vegetable peelings.

When the old woman sat on the porch to work on her book, she spent less time scratching her words across paper and more time staring without seeing across the frozen valley below.

Christmas Eve found the old woman sitting sadly on her porch with her book just a few pages away from the end and her year on the mountain about to end as well. She had given the hungry birds the rest of her bread and left her potatoes in a large bowl in the snow. All day she sat on the porch sighing, torn between going home to her family and staying on the mountain with her new one.

The wise spiders watched from inside the warm house, and thought of ways they could cheer the old woman who had become their friend. Aside from keeping the flies away in the summer, the spiders didn't feel like they had much to offer the old woman, being small and insignificant.

After much discussion it was decided that a small gesture is better than none, and they went to work.

As the night began to fall, the old woman sighed, got up from her porch and started inside to stoke up her fire. When she opened the door, she caught her breath in amazement. The spiders had woven their silvery webs all around the small pine tree, catching the setting sun in the gleaming strands.

Suddenly the old woman realized that she didn't need to worry about her forest friends, they had lived fine before she came and would continue on when she went back to her own. All their lives would be better for the small part they had shared.

The old woman lit her fire and sat on her couch to finish writing her book beneath the shining tree. Then she packed up the few belongings she had brought and prepared to go back. She opened the window so the little tree could get rain in her absence.

The spiders, being clever, knew that as soon as she left, so would the warm fire. They hid themselves around the pages of her book and prepared to travel back with her. When dawn came, the old woman traveled back down the mountain to her home and family.

Her children and grandchildren were overjoyed to see her, and the old woman's book taught many people how to be happier and live with the world rather than against it. The little spiders snuck out of the paper box and into her house where she let them live, after she discovered them, as long as they promised to remain out of sight under the floorboards.

The spiders were very good about keeping their promise except one day a year. Each winter the old woman would bring a pine tree inside to remind herself of her time in the woods. On Christmas Eve the spiders always snuck out during the night to spin their silver webs as a reminder that no matter how small and insignificant our talents may seem, we all have a gift to give.

This year, as you decorate your own tree with tinsel and shining things, remember the spider's gift and think of all the talents you have to give no matter how small and insignificant you may sometimes feel.

If you are very, very lucky, you may one day find a Christmas spider nestled in your own branches.

WHY WE WROTE THIS BOOK.

Christmas is a time of joy, but for many of us it is also a season of feeling inadequate and alone. Sometimes love and gifts get mixed up, and we worry if we don't give something wonderful we will not be loved.

Like the spiders in our story, we all have a fine gift to give. Sometimes it feels like it isn't appreciated, but when we give of ourselves with love then we have given something that is worth far more then anything that can be purchased.

This Christmas we hope you will find a way to give of yourself to the life all around you, and that the love you extend may come back to you multiplied.

Life is a beautiful thing, but only when we are.

About the author

Angela Yuriko Smith works for a weekly newspaper by day, blogs at Dandilyon Fluff and produces mainly children's books. Her published works, however, include fiction and nonfiction across multiple genres and she has been included in various anthologies and online publications. Mother of four, author of more, she is on a desperate search to find a cure for sleeping.

You can find her on Facebook as Angela Yuriko Smith, on Twitter as AngelaYSmith and visit her on her blog DandiFluff.com and AYWordSmith.com.

About the illustrator

Robin Wiesneth is an artist, writer, animal lover, story teller, sailor, traveler, and geek. She's fueled by wine and chocolate, inspired by the beauty and grace of animals, and obsessed with creating contagiously happy art and books.

She sometimes lives on the Gulf coast with her husband and badly behaving cat. Other times you can find her traveling across the USA in a motor coach, husband and cat in tow.

You can find her on Facebook and Twitter as ABrushwithHumor. Visit her blog at ABrushwithHumor.com for stories, new books, and general nonsense.

Made in the USA
Monee, IL
01 December 2022

19171026R00024